I don't know where the summ
someone had cancelled it and
friend and partner Ginny were stuck indoors as
the rain lashed at the windows. We both stared
outside in dismay with our arms on the
windowsill and our hands on our chins, it was
August and cold and rainy. Where had the
balmy hot sunny days gone?

"Well," Ginny said, "It's no good looking at the
rain lashing at the windowpane. I suppose we
had better get on with the housework. I don't
think we'll be going anywhere outside today
and the house needs a good clean from top to
bottom."

"Yes," I agreed, "we have enough shopping to
last until tomorrow and I see no other reason to
go out and get soaked. I'll give you a hand when
I have finished what I am doing on the laptop."

"Okay, Gail," Ginny replied. "I'll start upstairs and see you when you can come up." Ginny went off out of the living room and I heard huff and puff as she humped the old vacuum cleaner up the stairs. I felt guilty leaving my friend with all the work and I began rushing what I was doing so I could give her a hand. Ginny and I were in a formal relationship per sec, but it was also about sharing a house to keep down the cost of living. The arrangement left us both with a little bit of cash left to enjoy life. Ginny and I were very much alike we had bonded quite well and had a lot of things in common. We were both dominant ladies and into the kinky scene, indeed we first met in a fetish club in town. We got on really well, never argued and liked each other's company a lot.

However, today we're left to do our own housework as neither of us had a regular domestic slave to call upon. We have been looking for a 24/7 slave for some time, however, modern pressures make it very difficult for any prospective slave to take on such a role as it is likely their personal and financial lives would forbid such an arrangement. Both Ginny and I would settle for a local slave who could give up one or two days a week to come and be our skivvy, but there again there aren't enough genuine slaves out there and finding one who lives close enough to give us the time we need is a big ask and we haven't found such a person yet.

With these thoughts in my mind, I grabbed my rubber gloves and went up the stairs to find Ginny. Our house is really far too big for the two of us and we have three bedrooms which aren't used and still need to be cleaned. We also have two ensuite toilets a conservatory and other rooms which we don't use that much but still have to be kept clean.

The house is also costly to heat and the council tax is very high, but Ginny will not hear of talk of downsizing, so here we are scrubbing and cleaning the afternoon away. It is not a dignified activity for two Mistresses to be doing and these services should be done by a grateful and willing slave, except we don't have one, not today anyway.

I found Ginny lying on a bed in one of the spare bedrooms looking quite exhausted in her work frock and piny. She looked up at me with a look of despair and said:

"I'm too old for all this domestic work, Gail, what are we to do?" She asked.

"Well," I replied unsympathetically, "I have said time and time again we should downsize. I saw a nice little cottage on the edge of town for sale and it is in our price range," I said sitting on the bed beside her.

"I don't think we'll be able to sell this house," Ginny offered." It's an old house and has rising damp and a leaky roof. I don't think it will fetch enough money even to downsize and neither can we afford the repairs which will run into many thousands." I had to agree, and I too began to support a glum look as I sat there on the edge of the bed thinking.

"If only we had a decent, loyal, willing slave," I said, breaking the silence as we drifted off into deep thought.

"Well, Gail, you know the answer to that one, there aren't enough submissives living close enough and too few submissives want a 24/7 arrangement and those that do advertise for such a role are generally fantasising and not serious when it comes down to it. So your desire for a loyal willing slave is in the realms of fantasy I afraid."

"That means," I replied with resignation as I waved my duster graphically to demonstrate my point, "we had better get cleaning, the day is running away with us. With my comment, we both got up wearily from the bed and knuckled down to some more serious housework.

Over dinner that evening the topic of slaves came up again as we recovered from a day's slog.

"At least," Ginny said, "we have Graham coming to visit this weekend for a few hours of domestic work. I'll draw up a list of the things we don't want to do ourselves, like ironing for instance, and set him to work on those chores when he arrives. No point in having a dog and barking ourselves is there. We might as well make the best of him whilst he is here."

"I am grateful for Graham's services," I said, "but what's the use, he only comes once a month, if that, and he is only here for a caning, which is what he craves, so even his work is deliberately substandard to ensure he gets a hard spanking. For Graham, it is just a game."

"I know," Ginny conceded, "but at least he does do some work and you enjoy caning him and making his stand in the corner for a couple of hours before we pack him off home. He must get something out of the arrangement or he wouldn't come; would he?"

"If we had a couple of dozen more like him we might get by, but we only have a couple of slaves close enough to come just once a month," I said in resignation, and neither of them is very good at domestic work," I added.

"The odd thing is we live in a heavily populated area. You would think we would have plenty of slaves to choose from," Ginny remarked.

"That suggests there aren't enough of us who are genuine to go around. The websites are full of people, but I reckon only one percent are genuine submissives," I replied. "What does a Filipino maid cost?" I asked.

"They are cheap labour, but not cheap enough for us," Ginny replied with a sigh. "Also," she added, "you cannot beat them for bad work, and there are laws that forbid it."

"There must be a way," I said, feeling a little more enthused and upbeat; or was it unqualified optimism? The house is too big and we're getting too old to cope," I said in frustration, there must be something we can do.

"Let's think about it for a day or two and see what we come up with," Ginny answered. With that passing comment, we went to our respective beds. We did sleep together occasionally, but mostly we retired to our own rooms.

As there was no immediate solution to our domestic needs, the topic of slaves was dropped until after the weekend when we sent Graham home with a sore bottom from a very hard caning which I administered. I was usually tasked with chastising errant slaves as Ginny wasn't as keen as me. I actually got quite a thrill from giving a submissive, a good hard spanking. I loved everything about it the sound of the cane as it hit the target. I loved to watch the submissive squirm, wriggle and beg me to stop. One of my favourite things was to place the cane on the victim's bum then raise it and wait, whilst watching the slave's bottom contract as he anticipates the next stroke. I might do these two or three times before bringing the cane down, putting the slave out of his misery. I suppose you could say I was a sadist. Well, we all have our faults!

Whilst canning Graham was all good fun, it didn't solve our housecleaning dilemma. Although we had Graham slaving away the whole weekend, the house looked the same as it did before he arrived. The house was too big for a few hours of housework to make a visible difference. Also, as I said earlier, Graham would make deliberate mistakes to ensure he got his good hiding. Of course, we made him correct his mistakes, but that ate into the time available when we could have put him to good use doing something else.

What we wanted was a live-in proper, loyal, reliable slave capable of proper work, but how were we to achieve this? Was it an ambition too far; were Ginny and I being unrealistic?

Graham seemed quite happy with his weekend of servitude and went happily back to his home, which was a hundred or so miles north of us, leaving me and Ginny back to the unenviable task of doing our own housework. We both thought how undignified it was for two Mistresses to be mopped and sweeping our own house, but what needs to be done, has to be done whether we like it or not.

Ginny and I got on with life and between us decided to set aside Monday and Friday just to do housework chores. This on the surface seemed to work and we just knuckled down to the tasks that needed doing. Then one-day several months later I stepped into the kitchen to witness Ginny having a panic attack. I saw her throw a wet, soggy mop in the air and kick a bucket of warm soapy water across the floor until it landed at my feet soaking my legs almost up to my knickers as a tidal wave of water left in the bucket and surged up my legs.

"Ginny, what is the matter with you, you have soaked my legs?" I shouted, but she was too busy to hear me as she charged around the kitchen in a tantrum, knocking things deliberately off the worktops until she sank into a sobbing heap on the floor. In a rather dramatic and staged fit of pique, Ginny announced she could take no more and she considered herself not mentally or physically cut out for never-ending domestic drudgery.

"Aren't we all," I said to myself.

I wasn't overly sympathetic as to what else were we to do, let the house get filthy. We were hardly alone most ordinary people have to clean their own homes and it is a never-ending task. As the adage suggests:

"Women's work is never done."

Ginny remained sat on the soggy floor and seemed to brighten up for a moment and gave a weak smile, looked up at the ceiling and raised a hand, pointing a finger upward, as if she had received a message from God himself in a bolt of lightning.

"I have an idea," Ginny announced. "Come with me now," she urged, "down tools, and let's have a tea break and over a cup of tea and biscuits I shall tell you all about my brilliant idea." I followed Ginny downstairs, and I put the kettle on and sorted out some clean cups.

Chapter Two

I carried a tray of drinks and snacks into the living room where I found Ginny deep in thought. I placed the tray down and poured the tea for us both.

"So what is this wonderful idea you have to solve our domestic issues?" I asked a little frivolously as I couldn't see any solution apart from doing the work for ourselves with the occasional support of a willing submissive.

"You're not going to like what I have in mind," Ginny replied looking up at me seriously.

"Well, I'm all ears," I replied, taking a sip of my tea and helping myself to a current bun as I listened on.

"You'll agree, what we need is a live-in 24/7 domestic slave. Well, I have an idea if you approve," Ginny replied looking more enthused as she spoke.

"Yes," I agreed you're right, "and pigs may fly. We have been over this time and time again, there is no solution. I have been scanning the websites for months and nobody genuinely wants to be a full-time slave, not that I can find. They may exist, but they are eluding me."

"Yes, yes, yes, I know all this but I have another idea," Ginny replied, getting a little fed up with my negative attitude, "but hear me out."

I relaxed back on the sofa, taking my bun and tea with me to make myself comfortable for a long explanation from Ginny followed by a solution to our problems. Ginny fought hard before she spoke again as she formulated her response. I sensed I wasn't going to approve of what I was about to hear next from Ginny's hesitance to continue with the conversation. Then after an agonising pause that lasted many seconds, Ginny spoke up.

"The submissives that do visit us are very submissive aren't they, they do as they're told and take their punishment without complaint.

Most also work quite hard and are of genuine use to us.

"Yes, I agree," I remarked during a pause in the dialogue. "Go on," I urged, "is this leading us somewhere?"

"Most submissives," Ginny continued, "want to be led and controlled; they have no sense of direction and need to be dominated to bring out the best in them. Most submissives have told us they are more relaxed, happy and have a sense of freedom of responsibility when they are with us because they have a need to be bossed about."

"We know all this, Ginny. Come on, cut to the chase, or the remainder of our chores won't get done today," I said urging Ginny to get to the point.

"Well," Ginny continued. "Do you remember Ricky, the young lad about 25 years old who comes to us once or twice a year? He's a lovely lad very amenable, quiet and shy, a real darling."

"Yes, I do remember him," I replied, he has been recently hasn't he?"

"Yes," Ginny confirmed, "he came about two months back. He is one of our best slaves, he takes the work seriously and never deliberately makes mistakes and we have to try hard to find fault with his work."

"Yes, I remember well," I replied, "he is what I call a genuine slave in as much as he only wants to please. I believe, I added, "all genuine slaves only want to please their Master or Mistress, if they fail in that task, it really upsets them and they accept punishment as a means to improve themselves. But, I went on, where does that get us, what do you have in mind?"

"Do you also remember Ricky saying he has no family or friends where he lives? I also believe he is also out of work."

"Go on," I said becoming intrigued.

"Ricky is probably the most submissive of all our slaves, he is very pliable does exactly as he is told and is a little bit frightened of us; don't you think? Ginny asked.

"Yes," I replied, "he is without doubt the best slave we have. I just wish he could come more often.

"Okay," Ginny said, raising her voice slightly, "Ricky is due to come again in the next couple of weeks. I shall send him a reminder email and ask when he thinks he might get to us next. Because he lives so far away, he usually stops for a long weekend to make the journey worthwhile."

"Okay, you have my attention, so what is the bottom line; where are you going with this?" I asked.

"Why don't we kidnap Ricky and make him our full-time slave?" Ginny said without any change in her expression. I stood up, having finished my tea and currant bun and gave her an incredulous look.

"Come on, I said we have housework to do, "I seriously thought for a second you were about to say something sensible and constructive. I should have known better, we're just wasting valuable time when there are still stacks of housework to be done."

"Sit back down," Ginny insisted, "I haven't finished talking yet."

"Do you realise the penalties for kidnapping and keeping a non-consenting slave?" I replied mockingly. "There are newspaper articles and television programs about it all the time, it's called modern slavery and the sentences for wrongdoers are very high, but maybe you're right, there won't be quite so much housework in prison," I added, "but you'll still have shower rooms and halls to mop down. Also, don't forget your cell will need cleaning."

"I have thought about the legality of it all and it will be very difficult to prove abduction should things go wrong," Ginny replied.

"What makes you say that?" I asked.

"I have on my computer dozens of letters from Ricky begging to be our slave. In many of them, he expresses a desire to one day become a 24/7 slave. He has also requested we beat and tie him up. With those genuine emails, it will be difficult for Ricky to suggest he had been kidnapped and was non-consenting." Ginny said stopping to hear my response. "We can respond by saying we were just giving him what he asked for and we are all kinksters together."

"Yes, Ricky wants to be a full-time slave one day, but not now. What about the moral issue, we are forcing Ricky to be a slave against his will, and we'll have to live with that on our conscience. I am not so sure," I replied, not really warming to the idea. "I think we are building a world of pain for ourselves here. I hope you know what you're doing."

"Also, Ginny went on to say, how can we be accused of kidnapping him when he had willingly travelled over a hundred miles to see us? He is also very malleable and extremely submissive, when we tell him he is staying for good, he'll just accept his fate and maybe a 24/7 position is what he wants all along and just needs someone to make up his mind for him and give him that push. He might also be excited about being forcefully made to be our maid; lots do you know."

"He may act very differently to what we might imagine if he thinks he is being forced to stay against his will. I don't know," I added. "I really don't like the idea and I am not agreeing to anything just yet, only talking it through with you," I said, taking the proposition a teeny more seriously enough to discuss it more. I was about to ask some questions, but Ginny interrupted the flow of my thought processes by saying:

"It's simple, we will invite him for a long weekend, and when the weekend is over we tell him he is staying and is now our slave and property for life," Ginny said.

"Oh, as easy as that," I replied with my eyes rolling towards the ceiling. "But what if he doesn't want to stay, how do we hold on to him and where is his incentive to work hard for us if he is unwilling?" I asked.

"Ricky is extremely submissive, he wants somebody to take charge of him, a 24/7 position has probably been his lifelong dream, we are making it a reality for him" Ginny assured me.

"I see," I replied sarcastically, "so we are doing Ricky a service."

"That's right, you have got it," Ginny replied, failing to note I was speaking in jest, "One thing he hates and detests is being dressed up as a sissy maid if we take his male clothes away he wouldn't dare leave the house on his own," Ginny reassured me, "he'll be too embarrassed. I frilly maid's dress will be his jailer."

Okay, I added, "but what do we do with him when we have visitors?"

"We restrain him and put him in the cupboard under the stairs with a very severe warning about making any noises," Ginny answered. "So," she continued, "what do you reckon, Gail?"

Ginny decided for me and got up saying, "I have made up my mind for both of us, and we'll do this. I'll go and email him now inviting him down for this weekend."

With those words, Ginny darted off to her laptop and I stayed and the sofa in deep thought about Ginny's proposition. I concluded it would solve a lot of our problems and Ricky is very malleable and susceptible to doing as he is told. It is true, that he might just be looking for an excuse to be a lifetime slave to a couple of strict attractive Mistresses. He is very gentle, shy, and girly, although he doesn't realise it. He will probably go along with anything we say but I was a bit uneasy about it all, after all, we will be in effect breaking the law by holding Ricky by force.

Chapter Three

I let Ginny get on with her plans for Ricky and she managed to get the boy to agree to come next week for a long weekend stay, or at least that's what he thinks he's coming from. My attitude is that when he is here Ginny will see the sense in her hair-brained, ill-thought out idea and drop the matter there and then. I really didn't think she would go through with her plan, so I didn't worry too much about it and left her to her arrangements.

A couple of nights later I caught sight of Ginny through her bedroom door rifling through her wardrobe. I was quite interested to know what she was up to.

"Lost something?" I asked as I entered the room.

"No," Ginny said with a broad smile, "not as such, I am looking for the maid's costume one of our slaves left behind a couple of years back. It will be ideal for Ricky as it is more of a proper maid's uniform and not as fetish as a French Maid's outfit and if I find it, it will fit him well. Ricky will hate it all the same, as you know he's not keen on being feminised." Ginny said laughing. Ginny continued to look for the dress and pushed costumes up and down the rails until she found what she wanted.

"You're really going to go through with this, aren't you?" I asked, sitting on the edge of her bed. "I hope you know what you're doing. I really shouldn't be a part of your hair-brained idea."

"What do you think?" Ginny asked, dismissing my comments, holding up the dress for me to see. It was a nice costume and I could almost see Ricky in it, with a wig and a touch of makeup, he'll look so sweet."

I threw caution to the wind and started to fantasise about having a full-time maid who would do all our bidding and slowly warmed to the idea. Then I would jolt myself back to reality, if we do as Ginny plans we will be breaking the law and penalties for such will be very severe and if caught we'll almost certainly go to prison. Was it worth it just to have our own slave, I asked myself. Was doing our own housework really that bad?

Housework never kills anybody, and it is also good exercise and uses all the muscles in the body and will help us live longer. Having our own slave will only encourage us to be more sedentary, which isn't good for our long-term health.

I expressed my concerns to Ginny, but she had her mind set and by this time we were past the point of no return, in as much, as Ricky would have already set off from home to join us for the weekend. Of course, Ginny could change her mind when he arrives when she realises the enormity of what she proposes to do. If I go along with her plans, I am as guilty as she. I'll be an accomplice even though I don't entirely agree with what she is doing.

The fateful day arrived, and at about 5:30 pm there was a knock at the door. Ginny and I looked at each other as we sat in the kitchen.

Ginny gave a big grinning smile as she realised who it was and jumped up from her seat.

"I'll get the door," Ginny said, as she left the room to go down the hall to the front door. I listened on, and indeed it was the cheerful voice of Ricky as he struggled in with his bags.

"How are you Mistress and how is Mistress Gail?" He asked in his usual polite-mannered way.

"We are both well," Ginny replied. "You know where your bedroom is," she said to the young man, "go and put your bags in your room and we will have a cup of tea waiting for you in the kitchen when you return."

I could hear Ricky stomp up the stairs when Ginny reappeared in the kitchen. She went to the kettle to make Ricky and ourselves a cup of tea.

"He's here," she said all excitedly, our slave has arrived."

"Excuse me if I don't share your enthusiasm," I replied. "Are you sure you want to go through with this? It's not too late to change your mind you know, there is no harm done yet."

"Don't get so excited," Ginny reassured me, it will all go smoothly just you wait and see. Besides, Ricky won't be aware of our plans until he is due to leave on Monday, so you can relax for the weekend at least."

We both dropped the conversation when we heard Ricky descend the stairs and come into the kitchen. He was a lovely, harmless lad and greeted us with a beaming smile as Ginny passed him a cup of tea. I felt almost guilty for what we were about to do to such a harmless naïve young lad. IF only he knew he'd be running for the door.

"Come, take a seat at the kitchen table," Ginny urged, pulling back a chair for him.

"How was your journey, young man?" I asked passing him a tin of biscuits so he could take a couple.

"Not too bad, thank you, Mistress," Ricky replied nervously as he sipped his tea and took a biscuit. "The traffic wasn't too bad coming down, but I admit I'm a bit tired now, it was a long journey."

"You can relax," I said, "we won't be wanting much from you for the rest of today you can take it easy."

"We, Gail and I have decided to do things a little differently this time and we have decided you'll be our Victorian Maid for the whole weekend," Ginny said with a sarcastic smile. I could see Ricky's face drop as he hated the thought of dressing up as a maid, especially if it

31

was to be for the whole weekend. It is just as well that he doesn't yet know what is really in store for him.

"Do I have to be a maid," Ricky pleaded in a rather pathetic subdued voice.

"Yes, you do," Ginny said assertively. "We want to bring out the girly in you. When you have drunk your tea, you may go and shower. When you return to your bedroom you'll remain naked and wait for me, Mistress Gail and I will be up in about twenty minutes. Now, if you have finished your cup of tea off you go." Ricky began to stand, but I beckoned him to sit back down.

"Hold on for a second," I said, first we must think of a name for you, we can't call you Ricky when you're dressed as our maid, is there any girl's name you like," I asked, knowing the answer.

"No, Mistress," Ricky replied in a grumpy voice.

"Then we shall have to think of one for you," Ginny answered getting all enthused about naming our maid and it had all the excitement of choosing a name for a newborn baby. We sat at the kitchen table going through all the girl's names we could think of.

"How about calling her Isabella?" Ginny proffered.

"No, no," I replied it needs to be a name suitable for a maid, something short and sweet and easy to roll off the lips when we're ordering her about, something ending with a y or an ie."

Poor old Ricky had to listen to us discussing his new name as if he wasn't there or hadn't any say, which of course, he didn't. To add to his humiliation we insisted he come up with a name or two. Ricky struggled here as he didn't want to play this game and was reluctant to take part, however, I reminded him of some of the implements I had in my toy box if he didn't show more enthusiasm about her new persona.

"Okay," I said to Ricky, "if you can't think of any girl's name you like please tell us the names you don't like. Ricky hadn't thought this request through thoroughly and instantly built a rod for his own back.

"Mandy," Ricky blurted. "I had a cantankerous old aunt I disliked called Mandy," he added, "it made me cringe and gave me goose pimple every time I heard the name. It's a sickly name I can't abide it."

"That's a nice name," said Ginny, immediately picking up on Ricky's blunder and totally disregarding his opinions. "Don't you think Gail?"

"Yes," I do, it's a lovely name, I replied, "Mandy suits Ricky very well. I can imagine myself ordering Mandy around; the name rolls off the lips nicely and very suitable name for a maid.

"Then Mandy it is," Ginny confirmed, bringing the conversation to an end. I could see from Ricky's face he was far from pleased with his/her new name. "Right, Mandy off you go and have a shower. Take your time there is no rush."

Whilst Mandy was showering, I nipped into his room and removed all his male clothing including what he had in his case and locked it away. Ginny came into the bedroom and laid out the maid's dress and all the accessories on the bed ready for Mandy's return.

Ricky or Mandy as she is about to become, was a rather nervous lad, tall and lanky. He was also good-natured and very gentle and compliant. I had a tinge of guilt at what we were about to do to him, but this was tempered by all the housework we shall get done from now on. It will be so nice to just laze around leaving Mandy to potter about doing the housework on our behalf with the occasional flick of the riding crop to keep her motivated.

Mandy stepped back into the bedroom and blushed as she saw the two of us smiling at her with only a towel to save her modesty.

"Are we nice and clean now Mandy and refreshed?" Ginny asked. Mandy nodded. "Then, my girl let's start to get you dressed up and ready for work."

We spent about an hour dressing Mandy up until she met with our approval. The maid's costume fitted her like a treat. Once we added an apron, wig and frilly cap, she looked quite feminine.

We also taught her how to put on makeup and how to put on a wig and brush it into place. I was heartened when I realised through all the male bravado that she secretly enjoyed being dressed up and almost lapped up all the attention she was getting from us. He was definitely a girl at heart and needed someone to bring out his feminine side.

However, Mandy's enjoyment faded instantly when she realised all her male clothes were gone including those in his case. He looked up at us both with a questioning look as to why we had taken the clothes away. Before Mandy could ask, Ginny quickly took the words from his mouth and replied.

"Yes, all your male clothes have been taken away into safe keeping, we don't want you being distracted by anything masculine over the weekend we want you to fully immerse yourself into being our obedient, feminine and compliant Victorian Maid. You'll love it, trust me," Ginny added.

We took Mandy downstairs and fed her as we weren't going to make her do chores today as she already had a very long journey and would be very tired. We now had all the time in the world to fully break Mandy into how we wanted her to act and behave from now on, and a fresh start in the morning would be better after she had a good night's sleep.

After we had eaten I sent Mandy to bed, despite it being barely 8 pm, reluctantly, off she went to her bedroom, leaving Ginny and me on our own in the kitchen to discuss things further.

"Are you still going ahead with your plan, Ginny?" I asked with concern in my voice.

"Yes, of course, I am, we're committed now," Ginny replied with a confident smile. "You can see how malleable; he is putty in our hands."

"No, we're not committed there is still time for you to change your mind. If you do proceed, when do you propose to tell Ricky of his fate?" I asked.

"Mandy, you really must remember to call her Mandy; she's our slave for life now. There is no need to tell Mandy until she is due to go home, it's best she begins to settle into a routine first before we drop any bombshells," Ginny said standing. "Well, I'm off for an early night. It will be a busy day tomorrow as we start to break, Mandy in so she acts and behaves exactly as we want her to." I decided to join Ginny and do some reading in bed and followed her upstairs. In the morning, I found Ginny at the breakfast table, biting into some toast and marmalade.

"Where is Mandy it is almost 9 a.m.," I asked as I too put two slices of bread in the toaster.

"I am letting her lie in as she still must be exhausted from her travels yesterday," Ginny replied.

"That's very magnanimous you," I said sarcastically, "are losing your touch?" I asked.

"No just being reasonable, tomorrow Mandy will be up at 6 am sharp if she knows what's good for her," Ginny replied.

"The lull before the storm, well, I hope you're there to witness it, I'm not getting up at 6 a.m. For anyone," I replied jokingly.

"Here she is," Ginny announced as a very sleepy Mandy appeared in the kitchen doorway.

"Come in girl and make yourself some coffee and help yourself to some toast," I said, with a welcoming smile. I noticed her cringe when I called her a girl.

"Sorry," I'm late down," Mandy said apologetically.

"Never mind," Ginny said, you'll let you off just this once. I don't want you to think we're ogres, we know how exhausted you might be. Now relax and have some breakfast, we have a busy day ahead, but there is no immediate rush to get you started." Ginny said.

After breakfast, Ginny took control of Mandy whilst I sat at the kitchen table reading a magazine.

"Have you finished your breakfast," Ginny asked Mandy noticing an empty place and watching her drain the last of her tea.

"Yes," Mandy replied rather coyly.

"Do you want another cup of tea?" Ginny asked

"No thank you, Mistress Ginny," Mandy replied respectfully.

"Right then, step over here with me to our new notice board I made last night," Ginny said, standing from the kitchen table and making her way over to a far wall with Mandy quickly following on.

"On the notice board Mandy you'll see a rota of your work schedule. Today is Saturday and you'll see under Saturday the rota is sectioned off into three blocks morning, afternoon and evening, and in each of those segments you'll see your chores and duties, understand?" Ginny asked, looking at Mandy to see her reaction.

"Yes, Mandy replied.

"Good," Ginny said assertively, "and what is your first task for today?" Mandy stepped closer to the notice board and read aloud.

"I'm to clean the bath and shower rooms," Mandy looks back at Ginny for approval.

"Good girl," Ginny replied. "You know there are three shower rooms in this house don't you Mandy? Any questions before I send you off on your first task?"

"Um... Yes," Mandy replied, seeming a little confused.

"Go on," Ginny urged.

"I notice that the roster is for a week running from Monday to Sunday and the name Mandy is marked above every day on the work rota," Mandy replied with a perplexed look on her face.

"So?" Ginny replied.

"But I am only here for the weekend, until Monday lunchtime, then I must go home," Mandy explained.

"Don't worry about that," Ginny said unphased. "I'll explain it all to you later, off to the shower rooms with you. I'll send Gail up to check your work in an hour or so. Now go," Ginny said, raising her voice a notch.

With those commanding words, Mandy shot off for the stairs, leaving Ginny and me alone in the kitchen.

"Um," I murmured without explanation.

"Go on, Gail, spit it out, I know you're dying to say something, so let's hear it," Ginny said getting a little tetchy.

"Well," I replied nonchalantly. "It would seem you're encountering the seeds of dissent before you have dropped your bombshell on poor old Ricky," I answered.

"Mandy," Ginny said scolding me, "get used to calling her Mandy that will be her name for the rest of her life. As far as dissent goes, all will be explained to Mandy later on, there is no rush, it is only Saturday."

"Yes, that's what worries me is what, "Mandy's" reaction will be when you make your explanation."Ginny looked at her watch.

"It is time for you to go and check Mandy's work, to see if it is still up to her usual standard. Best to take your riding crop with you, she loves to see you holding it when you're doing your inspection, it will help her get into a submissive frame of mind," Ginny added passing me a crop. I went upstairs and found Mandy sitting on the edge of a bath daydreaming. She didn't hear me coming and jolted with surprise as I came into the bathroom.

"Have we finished?" I asked in my most disapproving voice. Mandy jumped to her feet and shivered in anticipation.

"Yes Mistress Gail," she crocked back in almost a stammer.

"Good, then let's see how well you have done. You must have done quite well to have time to sit and daydream," I said running my fingers over things exaggeratedly as I cruised around the bathroom.

"Oh dear, oh dear, you have lost your touch," I announced looking back at Mandy who was now cringing as she anticipated what might be coming next. "Let me show you what hasn't been done properly," I added, beckoning her with my finger to the basin.

"I can't see anything wrong," Mandy said feebly.

"You're questioning your Mistress?" I asked loudly. I grabbed her hand and ran one of her fingers around the base of the taps. "That's my girl is scale."

"I couldn't get it off," replied Mandy apologetically.

"Let me show you, before I show you, your other errors," I said going to the cabinet beneath the sink revealing the toilet cleaner. "If you squirt a small film of cleaner around the base of the taps, in ten minutes you'll be able to wipe the scale away. Now let's move on to the bath and shower unit. At the bottom of the bath, there is more scale around the anti-slip grooves. On the shower head, there is not only the scale but all manner of muck, this won't do Mandy. I shall have to punish you," I added bending the girl into the bath.

Holding her down with one hand on her back, I flicked up her skirt with the crop and pulled her tights and knickers down in a single movement. I love whipping a fresh unmarked bottom and watching the welts appear. I couldn't wait to get started, but first, it is obligatory to have a few practice whisks of the crop in the air for the sound effect as poor Mandy waited for the real punishment to begin.

"I accept you're not back into slave mode quite yet, so as I am a generous and kind Mistress I shall only give you six very hard strokes. Are you ready?" I asked. I always thought asking the submissive if they were ready to be punished was a silly thing to ask, of course, they weren't ready, but I would ask every time and every time and the slave would say yes.

I put the crop in my teeth, and with my free hand, I rubbed and caressed Mandy's bottom. So she would feel my warm, soft hand before the contrast of the sting of the crop bouncing off her bottom. I then placed the crop on her flesh and watched her tense her buttocks in anticipation of the first stroke. I liked to take my time, so the slave could feel the full benefit of the pain, there is no point in rushing these things. I loved the crack of the first stroke of the whip, it echoed around the bathroom and the girl's bottom flexed like a blancmange as the crop cut deep into her cheeks. When the six strokes were given, I released the hand from her back so Mandy could stand. I examined the welts and ran my fingers up and down them as that was something else I loved to do.

"Right," I said, "that's you sorted, and you may now correct your mistakes then go down to the kitchen and make yourself a cup of tea before looking to see what your next chore is on the roster."

I left Mandy to her amended chores and went down to the kitchen where I saw Ginny sitting at the kitchen table drinking tea and munching biscuits.

"I can see you have been enjoying yourself," Ginny said, pouring me a cup of tea.

"How?" I asked, "Could you hear the whisk of my crop down here, or Mandy's screams of terror."

"No," Ginny said. "I just need to look at you, your nipples are erect and showing through your blouse and your eyes are also glazed.

"Does it show that much?" I asked, sitting down and taking a sip of my cup of tea. "I left Mandy upstairs sorting out her mistakes with a suitably chastised bottom for her substandard efforts."

"I intend to tell Mandy she is staying here as our permanent slave on Monday morning," Ginny announced.

"You're leaving the bombshell to the last moment, then?" I asked.

"Yes, there is a method in my madness," Ginny assured me. "We get her to work hard for the rest of today and Sunday without any problems and it gives Mandy time to slip into a slave-like mentality, subspace, if you prefer, so she will be easier to control if she becomes problematic after hearing our news."

"You know I wanted a few days away to visit friends, Ginny, can I take them now," I asked.

"No," Ginny replied forcefully, "you're staying here to help me through this patch and provide moral support if things get difficult. Okay, Ginny conceded, "she might object for a day or two, then she will calm down and get on with her work like a good little girl, you'll see."

"I just wish I had your confidence," I replied.

Chapter Four

Mandy got on with her chores for the remainder of Saturday and Sunday without a hitch. I had to punish her a few times, but she would have been expecting that and disappointed if I hadn't chastised her for something. However, the day of reckoning arrived all too quickly and Monday morning soon came around. We had Mandy cleaning the kitchen in the morning and after lunch, she begged to leave us and go upstairs to get packed. I wondered how Ginny was going to handle this situation and I became very anxious as now that moment had arrived and poor Mandy would be told her life-changing fate at any moment.

"Come and sit down Mandy," Ginny said in an exaggerated kindly voice. "We have something to tell you. First, though, let me pour you a cup of tea." When Ginny had poured the tea, she offered Mandy a cream roll, which she avidly took without any persuasion.

"What is it you would like to tell me," Mandy asked with a mouth full of cream roll, which spit out of her mouth and ran down her chin.

"Would you like another cream roll?" Ginny asked, putting another roll on her plate," Ginny paused with a faint sigh as she grappled with how she was going to gently break the news to Mandy.

"How would you like to stay with us permanently as our maid?" Ginny asked, looking a little anxious as she waited for her reply. Meanwhile, Mandy grappled with her cream roll, which was disassembling itself as she ate and made a right mess. Ginny got up and brought over a kitchen roll for Mandy to wipe her face with.

Both Ginny and I sat on the edge of our seats waiting for Mandy's response. However, she had so much difficulty with her cream roll that Ginny needed to ask the question again.

"Oh, I don't know, it's a nice thought, but I think I am better off coming to you on an occasional basis," Mandy replied, not realising the importance of the question or quite what Ginny was getting at.

"Well, we think you'll be happier being our full-time maid. You enjoy working for us and you have a nice bedroom and we don't overwork you, do we?" Ginny replied.

"That's true," Mandy said finally finishing her cream roll and wiping down her face, but I want to go home now, please."

"Well, you can't leave Mandy," Ginny said forcefully, "We have decided for you, you'll be far happier here as our slave and maid." Mandy stood up and looked quite panicked as she paced frantically up and down the kitchen floor.

"But I have things to do at home, so I must leave now," Mandy said. "I am leaving now to pack, can I have my male clothes back now please."

"Sorry Mandy, your male clothes were taken to a charity shop last Friday," Ginny said.

"What about my money and train tickets?" Mandy asked.

"They have been confiscated," I said, feeling I too should have something to say and to back up Ginny.

"I'm going to call the police," Mandy said in a panic, not knowing what she should do next."

"Not on our telephone, you're not," Ginny said, "but you're welcome to leave, you know where the front door is. Go on then off you go," Ginny added shooing Mandy away with her hands.

Mandy started to go to the front door, but she was stopped in her tracks as Ginny reminded her how she was dressed:

"Before you leave Mandy," Ginny said, calling the girl back, "look at how you are dressed, do you really want to go outside dressed like that?" Mandy looked down at herself and looked completely at a loss to know what to do next. Mandy continued to head to the front door, but on route thought better of her predicament and realised there was no way she was going outside dressed as a Victorian maid. The embarrassment was too much for her to bear. At a loss to know what to do next, she returned to the kitchen door to plead with us once more.

"Come and sit down Mandy, things aren't as bad as they seem." I urged, tapping the chair where she had previously sat. Reluctantly Mandy came over to the table and sat down looking very agitated and uncomfortable.

"That's a good girl," I said in a soothing voice, "let's talk about your situation."

"Yes," said Ginny joining in the conversation.

"What do you have at home," Ginny asked, "that is worth going back to?"

"You don't have a job," I added, "therefore no work to worry about, no job to lose."

"Nor do you have any friends, so you're not sacrificing a social life." Ginny proffered.

"Our family to care for or be concerned about," I concluded.

"Now let's look at what you have here," Ginny said, "you have two beautiful Mistresses to bully you and keep you motivated. Seriously though, we will look after you and you'll become a part of our family."

"A nice comfortable room too," I added, "many slaves have to contend with sleeping on the kitchen floor, instead of a nice warm bed in a cosy room."

"I'm not your slave," Mandy insisted, "I want to go home now, so please get my clothes and my money for me. I know you have them somewhere" Mandy began to stand again with tears now cascading down her face until Ginny shouted at her.

"Sit down Mandy, I have explained you no longer have male clothing and your money has been spent and your train ticket refunded. So you're not going anywhere," Ginny insisted. Tears now began to pour uncontrollably down Mandy's cheeks as she looked at us with pure contempt and anger.

"Becoming our full-time slave, won't be so bad," I offered in a consolation. "You like it here with us, don't you?"

"Yes, but that was when I could come and go as I pleased. Now you want to turn me into a real slave for life," Mandy said crying tears of frustration and fear of the future. "I'm not staying, you can't keep me here forever," Mandy added with tears descending down her cheeks to such an extent it was making her dress collar wilt.

"We shall see about that, I have put a lot of thought into your incarceration and the dye has been set, there is no going back now," with those words Ginny got up and left the room, leaving me in charge. I went to the worktop and tore off a big strip of kitchen roll, came over to Mandy and wiped away the tears.

"It's best not to fight the inevitable. You'll soon settle down and things won't seem so bad," I said mopping up Mandy's tears.

Ginny returned to the kitchen with a sack full of objects and put them down on the kitchen table.

"Has she settled down?" Ginny asked me.

"No, I haven't," said Mandy indignantly, answering for me.

"Have you looked at the roster to see what your chores are for this afternoon," Ginny asked pointing to the notice board.

"I don't care what my duties are, I'm not doing them," Mandy said defiantly.

"Then you'll be beaten until you do?" I replied.

"It's no good threatening me, Mistress Gail, I am on strike, I refuse to do any work until you let me home," Mandy said folding her arms in defiance and starting to cry again.

"On strike are you Mandy, we'll see about that," Ginny said, pulling Mandy's chair out from under the kitchen table and sliding it with Mandy's still sitting in the chair over to a wall.

"You can sit there looking at the wall until you change your mind," Ginny said.

With Mandy no longer able to see us, Ginny put her finger to her lips and took from the sack two handcuffs and passed me one indicating that we should without Mandy realising handcuff her to the chair arms. Ginny and I tiptoed over and in a split second poor Mandy was restrained to the chair.

"Just shout when you want to start your chores," Ginny said, "you'll stay there until you do."

Mandy was left looking at a pale yellow wall. Ginny took from the sack a single-tailed whip and took it to show Mandy and she was warned if she moved a muscle, this is what she can expect to get. In my mind, although Mandy had the advantage of sitting in a chair, she had created a punishment for herself far worse than any whipping. The truth is sitting and looking at a wall with nothing else to do for an extended period is indeed a cruel punishment.

We soon realised Mandy was a stubborn individual and an hour had passed and she hadn't moved a muscle. However, we knew this couldn't last, if for no other reason sooner or later she needed a pee if pure boredom hadn't weakened her first. It was around 10 am when Ginny slid Mandy's chair over to the wall, now it was nearly lunchtime and Mandy had not protested or moved a muscle, she quietly sat there staring at the wall. The boredom for her must have been excruciating.

"She'll weaken when we start cooking," I whispered to Ginny so Mandy couldn't hear us talking about her.

"I'll cook bacon and eggs that should start the girl's tummy rumbling. She can't keep this up too much longer," Ginny assured me.

Oh yes she could, the smell of lunch hadn't made her capitulate or stir in her seat, she sat there steadfastly refusing to flinch. Lunch came and went, and now the light outside was beginning to go down. The silence in the kitchen was finally broken it took Ginny and me so much by surprise we both jumped when Mandy suddenly and unexpectedly spoke.

"I need to go to the toilet Mistress," a voice said from the wall.

"Okay, does that mean you'll begin your duties now, you'll have to work late tonight to catch up," I asked.

"No," replied Mandy defiantly.

"Then you can pee in your seat and when we do release you, you can clean up the mess after a hard caning," Ginny replied angrily, as she realised that taming Mandy wasn't going to be such a piece of cake as she imagined.

"I can hold on," Mandy replied with determination.

"Good and have the decency to wait until we have had dinner before you foul the kitchen floor," Ginny said as equally defiant. "We're having a leg of lamb tonight with all the trimmings."

"Do you like mint sauce Mandy, you can join us if you decide to end your protest and accept your destiny," I asked.

"No thank you," was Mandy's defiant reply.

"When dinner was cooked, Ginny and I carried our food next door into the dining room. Ginny returned and switched off the kitchen light, but she left the adjoining door open so we could keep an eye on Mandy. I tiptoed over and peeked around the door to see poor Mandy sitting there, rigid in the dark undeterred. When I returned to the dining table, I whispered to Ginny:

"What are we going to do, Mandy isn't weakening?" I asked.

"Nothing that's what we do, nothing at all," Ginny replied. "She can stop there the night if she wishes, sooner or later she will need to eat or go to the loo. She can't keep this up much longer, besides the boredom of doing absolutely nothing for hours on end must also be taking its toll."

We momentarily forgot about Mandy and carried on with our food. I poured Ginny and me a glass of wine, and just as I did so I heard a pathetic voice from next door.

"I give in," said a parched Mandy who was thirsty, hungry and busting for the loo. "I will be your slave," she added wriggling on her chair. I realised she couldn't hold on much longer without the toilet and took the handcuff keys from Ginny and rushed over and released her.

"Go on off to the toilet quickly," I urged, "we'll talk when you return." I had never seen anyone move so quickly in all my life she disappeared in a flash slamming the kitchen door behind her as she rushed upstairs to the loo. Mandy was gone an age before she finally returned to us in the dining room.

"Curtsey," Ginny demanded, "when you come into a room with your Mistresses present you give a respectful curtsey, do you hear?" Ginny said in an uncompromising voice. Mandy stood and gave a quick but reluctant bob to please Ginny.

"Go and help yourself to a coffee and there is a dinner in the oven, bring them here and sit with us," I said, shooing her away. A short while later, Mandy returned with a tray of food and a coffee.

"In future Mandy," I said in my authoritative voice you'll eat in the kitchen by yourself, but this evening we want to chat and now you accept your future we need to discuss some of the house rules so you fully understand your obligations."

"I take it," said Ginny, "you have accepted your future as a life-long maid/slave for Gail and me?"

"Yes," Mandy said with a mouthful of food. The poor girl must have been starving, though we were not entirely convinced about her reply. I for one wasn't ready to believe Mandy was ready to be passive and compliant so soon and she'll need further breaking in. We discussed the rules and protocol, the usual stuff, no sitting on furniture, eyes cast down and lots of curtsying et cetera to keep her busy and submissive. After Mandy had a second helping of food and another coffee, we sent her to bed. When Mandy had left us, I turned to Ginny and said:

"Mandy isn't broken in," I said, "she will still try to leave if we give her half a chance."

"I know," Ginny replied, reluctantly agreeing with me.

"What can we do to stop her leaving?" I asked. "We can't let her go now we'll be in all sorts of trouble,"

We'll have to double up on security," Ginny said.

"The good thing is we rarely have visitors calling unannounced, and nearly always, we know when we are having guests. That gives us time to lock Mandy in her bedroom or something when we are entertaining," I said, giving the matter some thought.

"Yes, I also thought we might put digital locks on the doors both inside and out then, we don't need to run the risk of leaving keys lying about, or forgetting to take them with us when we go out," Ginny suggested. I will ring around a few locksmiths tomorrow."

"Don't worry," Ginny added, "Mandy is okay once we have broken her in and she accepts her situation isn't going to change."

Chapter Five

Ginny was far too complacent and Mandy had far from given up on trying to leave. The very next morning while Ginny and I waited in the kitchen for Mandy's arrival for breakfast she failed to appear. I wasn't as surprised as Ginny was, but we were both very angry that Mandy should be playing up so soon.

"I had better go upstairs and try and find out what has happened to her," I said going towards the staircase. When I arrived upstairs, I went straight to her bedroom to find she wasn't there and the bed was left unmade. I assumed Mandy might still be in the bathroom and tried there, to find the bathroom empty. I shouted her name with no response. I went to the top of the stairs and shouted down to Ginny:

"We have a problem, Ginny; you had better come up here."

I heard the thud of Ginny's shoes as she came upstairs and when she arrived I said in a concerned voice.

"I can't find Mandy she's not in her bedroom or the bathroom."

"Okay," we'll search the whole house, she can't have gone far. I have locked all the outer doors and windows, she has to be somewhere in the house," Ginny assured me. "I'll look downstairs and you have a thorough search up here, look in every room and all the cupboards," Ginny added. After a hurried search, Ginny and I met up halfway up the stairs.

"She not up here," I said with a bit of a panic, "I've searched everywhere."

"I have searched everywhere downstairs too. We must have missed something, there is no way she can leave the house," Ginny assured me. "I know where I didn't look in the airing cupboard; it is plenty big enough for Mandy to hide."

"What is the point in hiding, she has to come out sometime," I said to Ginny.

"I reckon if we can't find her, Mandy will wait until tonight, look for our keys and sneak out the front door." Ginny proposed.

Dressed as a Victorian Maid?" I replied.

"If she is still in a maid's dress, let's go and look in the linen cupboard," Ginny said creeping back downstairs and beckoning me to follow her.

Just as Ginny and I approached the airing cupboard we heard a faint cough and we knew she was in the cupboard somewhere. We crept up and Ginny pointed to the cupboard key and put her finger to her lip to stop me from talking.

"Gail, you naughty girl, don't we keep this cupboard locked?" I realised what Ginny had in mind, and I went along with the pretence.

"Yes we do, I am so sorry Ginny, I must have forgotten," I replied.

"Well we had better lock it now," Ginny said twisting the key and trying the door.

Despite Mandy being clearly aware of her fate, she still refused to admit she was in the cupboard, so Ginny and I walked away. When we were out of hearing Ginny said we'll leave her in the cupboard until dinner time. It will be dark, hot and miserable in there, when we return she will be begging to come out.

So we left poor old Mandy in the dark with no means of escape and Ginny and I went back to the kitchen to make a brew.

We left poor old Mandy in the cupboard for about two hours with no means of escape, and then we thought it was time to go and have a stern word with our errant maid. After lunch, Ginny and I went down to the airing cupboard and we heard shuffling from inside. Ginny unlocked the door and we saw the pathetic sight of Mandy curled up amongst the pipes and immersion heater. She looked very hot, sweaty and blinking furiously from the bright light of the opened door.

"Why are you in the cupboard, pray tell me why do you dress in a pink t-shirt and shorts instead of your uniform?" Ginny said in a stern voice which had Mandy cringing.

"Come out you come," I added. "Take yourself to the kitchen and make yourself a drink and we will have a nice long chat and we can also decide on your punishment." Both Ginny and I followed a stiff and sweaty Mandy to the kitchen. Mandy went nervously to the kettle. She was barely able to stand up straight after being bent over double in the cupboard for so long.

"While you're at it you can make Gail and me a coffee too," Ginny said maintaining her authoritative voice.

When the drinks were made and Mandy brought a tray over to the kitchen table, I said:

"Sit down and explain yourself. Ginny and I want to know what's so fascinating about the airing cupboard." Poor Mandy didn't know what to say and just sat there looking pathetic as she struggled to say anything at all.

"As you can't seem to speak, I'll tell you what you were doing in the airing cupboard," I said, saving Mandy the agony of explaining herself. "You were trying to escape, weren't you? This will explain the clothes you're wearing."

"You were hoping to sneak out of the house when we had given up looking for you," Ginny concluded for me.

"Well my girl you'll need to be punished severely so you don't try such a thing again," I said. "In the meantime, when you finish your tea you may get on with your chores, when I am ready to give you your chastisement, I will find you," I said.

"What about lunch?" Mandy asked looking very sheepish.

"What lunch? If you wanted lunch you should have been here instead of examining the airing cupboard plumbing," Ginny chirped dismissing the question out of hand.

A subdued and chastened Mandy set off to change into her uniform and commence her household chores knowing punishment would be on the agenda when she has finished. In the meantime, I had the onerous task of thinking of a suitable punishment that may just deter Mandy from future thoughts of escaping to freedom. Especially as she knows in her heart of hearts she wants to remain with us in perpetual servitude as all good, obedient maids should.

At around nine pm Mandy reappeared hot, tired and stood wearily to attention at the door for permission to enter.

"Mandy goes to the kitchen and you find a hot meal in the oven when you have eaten it and had a drink report to me here in the living room, we have unfinished matters to attend to," I said pointing back at the kitchen. Mandy turned slovenly on her heels and made her way back into the kitchen.

When Mandy returned from her late dinner in the kitchen, she stood in the doorway of the living room looking very sheepish as she fidgeted while awaiting a response from me or Ginny.

"Come here Mandy and stand before me," I said in my most serious voice as I pointed to a spot at my feet. Mandy shuffled over and stood to attention on my feet. I could see her physically quiver at the thought of what I might do to her next.

"We are very disappointed in you Mandy, you promised us you would not try to escape and you have let both of us down and that needs severe punishment, doesn't it Mandy?" I asked. Mandy bowed her head in subdued shame and nodded in agreement with me.

"Come with me upstairs to my bedroom," I demanded paving the way. "I have some things arranged on my bed for you," I said as we ascended the stairs. Outside my bedroom, I paused for effect as Mandy was riddled with anticipation about what awaited her. Slowly, I pushed the bedroom door open:

"After you," I said ushering Mandy into the room. I stood behind her as Mandy viewed the items I had put out in her honour. I then stepped to her side to also look at the array of implements I had put on the end of the bed for Mandy to see. "Impressive isn't it, all specially selected for you?" I added. "Now young lady undress, everything off the lot. I want you as naked as the day you were born. I shall sit on the couch until you're ready."

Mandy slowly and reluctantly removed all her clothing, folding each item up neatly and placing them on a small table at the side of her couch. When she was undressed, I stood and came over to the girl. I pulled the couch up closer to the end of the bed.

"Sit," I bellowed. Poor Mandy cringed at the volume of my voice and sat back down again.

"I am not quite ready for you yet you may sit here and look at all the delights I have for you later. As you can see there is a mixture of canes, floggers, paddles, whips and crops. We'll start from the left using the mild implements and work along to the right where we have the beasts." I stopped speaking to see Mandy's reaction as she surveyed all the goodies on the duvet. "You may pick them up and handle them if you wish, but don't change the order or you'll be in bigger trouble. I'll be back shortly to sort you out."

Then I left the room leaving Mandy to stew looking at the implements while I returned downstairs.

"You're back," Ginny said, "that's quick I didn't hear a sound."

"I haven't started," I assured Ginny, "I have left Mandy to look at the implements and allow her to become riddled with expectant anticipation. By the time I return, she'll long to get the beating over and done with."

"How long will you leave her to stew?" Ginny asked with curiosity,

"Let's see its 8 pm, she can wait until 9:30 pm, she should have stewed enough by then and will almost welcome a good beating." That made Ginny chuckle and whilst she was laughing at poor Mandy's misfortune I left the room and came back with a bulging shopping bag,"

"What's in there?" Ginny asked.

"You'll see later another little surprise for Mandy.

"I can't wait to see what it is," Ginny replied.

At 9:30 pm I got up from my armchair in the living room and said to Ginny before leaving the living room:

"I had better go and sort Mandy out, she has waited long enough. It's time to put the girl out of her agony."

"Have fun, don't be too gentle with her, she needs a good hiding," said Ginny with a smile as I left the room.

Chapter Six

I opened the bedroom door and Mandy was still sitting looking at the equipment on the bed. Her eyes pleaded with me to get on with her punishment and put an end to her agony.

"You must be dying for a pee Mandy," I said, "go to the bathroom and return to me immediately," I demanded. Mandy was bursting, and like lightning, she shot out of the bedroom door. When she returned, she saw me holding a leather paddle the first implement in the row of implements. Mandy looked very sheepish as she stepped back over to the end of the bed where she saw a pillow had been placed.

"Come here," I barked and bend over the pillow I had put out for you. Mandy did as she was told and bent over the pillow and bed, and then shuffled a bit to make herself comfortable.

"That's it," I said make yourself as comfortable as you can, as you'll be here for some time. With that comment, the relative silence was rocked by the loud crack of the paddle coming down on Mandy's bottom. Her bottom quivered like a blancmange, followed by a whimper which got louder with each stroke. Next came the floggers which made more noise than pain, which gave Mandy a small respite. However, her discomfort soon returned with twelve strokes of a thin whippy riding crop. Now Mandy was hurting and wriggling to deflect the pain of each contact of the crop. I was pleased to see the tears begin to roll down her tortured face. Mandy was beginning to understand what real punishment is about.

"We still have a little way to go," I advised Mandy, "we haven't got to the canes yet," I said, picking up the first cane and whisking it a bit in the air for effect which was working nicely on Mandy's nerves as her bottom creased and quivered with each sample flick of the cane. Then I began for real which had Mandy begging, crying and squirming for respite.

"The last ten," I said with the senior rattan cane, this will have you jumping about and begging for mercy."

"I started the ten strokes which bit deeply into Mandy's already bruised bottom, which indeed had her jumping about on the bed. I had to constantly tell the girl to resume her punishment position.

"Are you going to try and escape again?" I asked halfway through the ten strokes. "Have you accepted your fate and you are now our slave and maid for life?"

"Yes Mistress, yes Mistress," was the muffled reply. "I want to be your maid; you'll have no further trouble from me."

"Good, then let's proceed with the last five strokes, you may count these and say thank you Mistress Gail after each one. If you forget the score, we will begin again. Understood?" I asked.

"Yes Mistress," Mandy just managed to say before the first of the much harder strokes landed on her bottom creating deep angry red welts. "Thank you, Mistress Gail," was the reply before I continued with the next stroke.

When the beating was complete Mandy stood, and I got a tissue, wiped her eyes and said in a motherly way:

"There, there," it's all over now Mandy. "Although I have one more surprise for you, don't worry it won't hurt," I assured her. I picked up the shopping bag and said. "Right Mandy go back to the toilet and I'll see you in your bedroom and don't forget to take your clothes."

I waited in Mandy's bedroom for Mandy to return when she did so, I ordered her to put her day clothes away and to don a nightie. When Mandy was dressed in her nightie, I ordered her into bed. Then I took from the shopping bag a chain about 18 inches wide, on each end it had a padded leather cuff.

"Do you know what this is for?" I asked Mandy.

"No," was the confused reply.

"I bet you have a shrewd idea what it might be for?" I said pulling back the bed covers and pulling out her right foot. "One end is for your foot," I said attaching the cuff and padlocking it and the other end is to go around the bed leg which I did by fastening another padlock. The idea is that I shall know exactly where you are in the morning. As fascinating as the airing cupboard is, I don't want to see you in there again and I don't want to find you missing either," I added checking the security of the chain. "So it only leaves me now to wish you good night and I hope your sore bottom doesn't keep you awake, lots of work for you to do tomorrow. Nite, nite," I added as I switched off her light and closed the bedroom door leaving Mandy to settle down and sleep.

In the morning I arrived in Mandy's bedroom at 7 am to unshackle her from her bondage. I unlocked the chain from the bed and let it dangle loosely.

"Turn over," I demanded, "let's take a look at your bottom." Mandy turned over and the bottom was black and blue and looked extremely sore. "I hope your bottom didn't keep you awake?" I asked

"For a while Mistress Gail," Mandy replied.

"Your bottom will be sore for a few days yet," I advised Mandy, now go to the bathroom wash, makeup, put on your uniform and come down to the kitchen. I was about to leave when Mandy stopped me with a question.

"Mistress," she chirped shyly, "What about the chain, it's still cuffed to my leg.

"I know," I replied, "we'll sort that out when you come downstairs." With those words, I left Mandy to get herself ready for the day. Around half an hour later I heard the shuffling of a chain come towards the kitchen. In came Mandy with the chain and vacant cuff trailing behind her. Ginny smiled as she surveyed the pathetic sight.

"Come here and stand before me," I said pointing to the spot where I wanted her to stand. When she arrived, I picked up the vacant cuff, put it on the other leg and fastened the padlock.

"There," I replied with satisfaction that would stop you from running off. Have a little walk around the kitchen for us," I demanded. Mandy quickly discovered she was only able to take small dainty steps and the chain was making such a noise we could hear her coming a mile off. I was sure this measure would dull any thoughts of escape from our clutches.

"That's the surprise you talked about last night," Ginny announced as she watched Mandy awkwardly shuffle around the kitchen.

"Yes," I replied, "I'm afraid we cannot believe or trust Mandy's word, so the chain will ensure she doesn't escape. I have also ordered new digital locks for the exterior doors. I could see Mandy's mind working furiously on how she could cope with this new development and still secure her escape when she was ready for her next attempt.

"There is no escape now Mandy, accept it, and get on with your life as our maid," I advised. "If you work on becoming our loyal and reliable maid we'll treat you much better, so that is something for you to look forward to, isn't it?."

Mandy ate her breakfast, went to the notice board and checked the roster for her day's chores before leaving me and Ginny sitting at the kitchen table.

"Do you think she will behave now?" Ginny asked.

"No," I replied, "she's still looking at ways to escape, we'll need to be vigilant and keep a sharp eye on her at all times, until she realises how hopeless her situation is and accepts her fate, but it won't happen overnight."

The rest of the day went well Mandy got on with her work which was to an acceptable level, so I had no need to punish her for any errors. Ginny remarked that finally our maid was accepting her fate and knuckling down to the tasks we set her. The next two days were much the same and we began to get less nervous about Mandy's desire to escape our clutches. Five days on from Mandy's last attempt to escape we once again had problems with her. The incident happened around 11 a.m. I had just come down from upstairs and I saw Ginny going down the hall to the front door. I thought nothing of it; Ginny often went out late morning to the convenience store a street away to get milk and anything else we were running low on. Just as Ginny reached the front door, I shouted:

"Bye, see you in a bit." Ginny didn't turn she just grunted something under her breath and I just thought she was too busy to reply properly, so I left her to it, went on into the kitchen and who did I see, but Ginny stood there at the sink.

"How come you're here?" I said. "You have just left to go to the shops." As I spoke I realised what had happened.

"No," Ginny replied, we don't need anything from the shops today."

"Then who did I see go to the door?" I asked perplexed.

"Oh no," we both chanted at the same time.

"It's Mandy escaping I said in horror, "and she is wearing your coat and clothes."

"We had better get over her before she gets too far," said Ginny dropping her potato peeler on the floor and dashing out of the kitchen and down the hall with me following on behind, grabbing her coat as she went.

"How long ago did you see her leave?" Ginny asked as she got to the front door.

"Seconds ago, just before I spoke to you," I replied as we both stepped outside into the cool autumn air.

"You go one way and I'll go the other," Ginny said darting off to the left leaving me to search for the right. I quickly got into a sprint and I must have run a good mile but I couldn't see Mandy anywhere. We didn't think for a moment she would try to leave dressed as a woman, but of course, she wasn't in her maid's costume but dressed in Ginny clothes and would look very passable to all who encounter her. It looked as if she had pulled it off this time and escaped from us.

Tired from my sprinting I walked slowly back to the house feeling very dejected and forlorn. As I approached the house I saw Ginny holding Mandy by the ear as she dragged the girl back to the house. I felt so relieved we had found her, I didn't want to contemplate the amount of trouble we would be in if Mandy went straight to the police. I entered the house and saw Ginny in the hall looking very frustrated.

"Where is she?" I asked. "What have you done with Mandy?"

"She is back in the airing cupboard until we decide what to do with her," replied Ginny.

"Why the airing cupboard," I asked.

"It was the first place I could think of to put her, besides she likes it in the airing cupboard." I laughed and asked:

"Where did you find Mandy?"

"I ran as fast as I could, I assumed she would head for the railway station. I knew she might have some money as I found some missing a few days ago, so I assumed she had enough to buy a railway ticket home."

Ginny and I walked into the kitchen and I put the kettle on and sat Ginny down as she was still panting and wheezing from all the running.

"Go on," I said as I dipped a tea bag in our mugs, what happened next?"

"As I approached the station I saw what looked like my coat and assumed it was Mandy as she was the same height and had Mandy's distinctive gait. She was just about to go up the steps and into the station. I ran a bit faster and as she reached the top step, I grabbed her handbag and pulled it from her grasp breaking the strap to ensure she had no funds. I then gripped her arm quite tightly and started to drag her back unceremoniously down the stone steps. God knows what people thought was going on. Mandy now knew the game was up and came back with me to the house without too much fuss."

"Oh good," I said, "and what do we do with her now? Do you know how she got the cuff and chains off her feet?" I added. "I'm surprised about that; I thought that would stop her from going anywhere."

"They are in the hallway she cut the leather cuffs with a kitchen knife," Ginny replied.

"Well," I replied, "that will require extra punishment as they cost a fortune to buy. I bought leather cuffs for her comfort, I have some uncomfortable metal ones I can use that will stop the same from happening again, I would like to see Mandy cut through steel," I said, showing my annoyance by waving my arms in the air with exasperation.

"How are you going to punish Mandy?" Ginny asked.

"I don't know," I replied thoughtfully. Whatever I do for punishment it will have to be very, very severe."

"Well," Ginny replied, "I don't want to see her again today she can stay in the cupboard until tomorrow morning."

"What about food," I asked, "she hasn't eaten a thing today."

"What food?" Ginny replied without a flicker of concern." She doesn't deserve food, starving until morning will be my contribution towards her severe punishment."

In the morning I got up a little earlier than usual and went downstairs to the airing cupboard and let Mandy out. I let her go straight to the toilet, wash, makeup and I told her to get out of Ginny's clothes, put them in the washing machine and see me in the kitchen when she was more comfortable and fit for work.

I watched her strip off her clothes as she put them in the washer and came over and stood before me in her bra and panties.

"What are we going to do with you, Mandy?" I said in frustration, "Well, you had better make yourself some cereal and a cup of tea before Ginny comes downstairs as she had stale bread in mind for your breakfast. Then, my dear, we need to think about your punishment as the last session obviously wasn't severe enough to deter you from escaping."

"I'm sorry Mandy," Mandy sputtered. "I won't try to escape again I promise. I'll behave, you'll see."

"I don't believe you, I think you're sorry for what is going to happen to you next and sorry for a night in the cupboard, but not sorry for attempting to escape, this is what we need to address," I said, pouring myself another drink. "I am also angry you cut your leather cuffs off did you know what they cost my girl?" I added indignantly. "Money doesn't grow on trees you know."

By this time Ginny arrived in the kitchen and stood silently frowning at Mandy with her arms in a dominant pose on her hips. It was several seconds before she spoke.

"So," Ginny said to me, you let Mandy out of the cupboard, and," she added picking up the empty cereal bowl, "you have fed her as well. Pampering Mandy is what is giving up all these problems. Spare the rod and spoil the slave, that's what I say. Maybe I should take over the discipline in this house. I'll make sure she doesn't want to escape again, I can assure you of that."

"How do you intend to punish Mandy?" Ginny asked me.

"I'll decide after I have had my breakfast," I replied. "I'll promise you Ginny it will be very severe," I assured the woman.

"Good," Ginny replied bluntly, "for if she tries to escape again, I'll deal with her, she will find I'm not such a pussycat like you are Gail," she said staring at Mandy to the point I could see the poor girl physically cringe at the thought and was glad it was me who was going to meet out the punishment.

"Mandy," I barked, now you have had a drink and something to eat, go over to the kitchen wall and stand perfectly still with your hands at your side, palm open and touching your thighs. You will not move a muscle, not as much as a twitch, until I tell you, do you understand Mandy?" I asked.

"Yes Mistress Gail," Mandy replied, almost inaudibly as she rushed over to the wall and stood to attention as requested.

"Is your nose touching the wall?" I asked.

"Yes Mistress Gail," was the reply.

"Good," I replied, "you may stay there until I tell you to move and not before."

I sent Mandy to the wall as I still had no idea as to what to do about Mandy's main punishment, but whatever I was to decide it needed to be very severe to deter the girl from wanting to escape again.

Chapter Seven

I let Mandy stand her nose against the wall until almost midday to warm her up to the prospect of even greater punishments. Finally, I told her to come away from the wall and stand before me as I sat at the kitchen table. When Mandy arrived I showed her my new cuffs and chain.

"The cuffs are metal Mandy, you won't be able to get these off and they lock with an Allen key which I have in my hand," I said, showing her the key. "This is the only one of the sort in the house and I shall keep it on my person at all times." When I finished speaking, I asked

Mandy to put one foot on the runner of my chair so I could attach the cuff to her ankle and then asked for her other foot.

"If you look over at the side of the kitchen door you'll see a bunch of chains lying there pick it up and come with me," Mandy picked up the heavy tangle of chain and followed me to the back door.

"Right young lady untangle the chain and bring me one end I said sitting on a nearby chair as she sorted the chain out and brought me one end.

"Put one end around the water pipe and attach this padlock," I ordered passing Mandy an open padlock. "Then you show that the padlock is closed properly. Mandy demonstrated she had fastened the padlock onto the chain correctly. "Now open the back door, feed the rest of the chain through the cat flap and attach it to the centre link on the chain you're wearing on your ankles.

I took Mandy out into the garden to the sound of the long chain rattling behind her. We stopped at a sheltered corner of the garden and I said:

"We are doing some gardening today Mandy," I said, showing her about ten square feet of eighteen-inch tall stinging nettles. Mandy looked at me and gulped at what I was going to say next.

"You have guessed Mandy, clever girl, yes you're right I want you to clear all the nettles away and put them in the compost container. You get started and when you're done come and knock on the back gate. Enjoy yourself, the sun is shining," I concluded as I was about to walk away. "Oh," I turned to say, "Bring the last bunch of nettles with you when you come to the back door." I took a couple of steps as I walked away to stop when Mandy asked.

"Mistress Gail," she cried pathetically, "can I have some gloves please to wear to pick the nettles?"

"Your hands Mandy, use your hands, I'm not going to spoil you with gloves. Now get started I expect the job to be done in an hour or so," I replied dismissing the girl and continuing to walk back to the back door.

After about an hour a very upset, dirty and grubby Mandy appeared at the back door clutching some nettles. She passed them to me.

"Oh, no," I said rejecting the nettles, "wait there, until I put my rubber gloves on." When I made a show of putting on my yellow rubber gloves, I took the nettles and I got Mandy to follow me back down the garden. We stopped at a summer house and opened the door for the maid to go in ahead of me.

"Strip off Mandy, everything the lot. Fold the clothes nicely and hand them to me. Mandy did as she was told and stood there slightly shivering from the cold. "Good," I replied, now open your legs."

"I rubbed the nettles liberally around poor Mandy's private parts and then up and down the tender parts of her anatomy including under the armpits. Then I picked up her clothes and went to the summerhouse door and passed through it, locking Mandy naked inside as she shivered and looked very sorry for herself.

I returned to the kitchen and told Ginny what I had done which met with her approval.

"How long is she to stay in the summer house?" Ginny asked.

"Well," I said, "she was shivering when I left, so I don't want her to become ill, but a lesson must be taught, so I'll leave her to dark."

"Will that be an end to her punishment?" Ginny asked.

"Not quite, when I collect Mandy she will be cold, so I'll take a cane with me to warm her up a bit before allowing her to come back inside the house. I will take her clothes so she can quickly dress after her caning as I say I don't want the girl to fall ill, as an ill maid will be a burden."

The latest punishments seemed to subdue Mandy, and she did settle into her role as our slave and did some really good domestic work. We did think all our troubles were over and we finally managed to break Mandy in and reduce her to a servile and passive slave willing to serve her two elegant and demanding

Mistresses. I kept up her punishments to help keep her submissive, but as the weeks rolled on I could see she was once again becoming dissatisfied and edgy and I thought she may once again be looking at ways of escape.

I couldn't see how she could achieve her aims as she now wore metal cuffs habitually and a short chain, so she could hardly run away. The doors were now locked digitally so no keys to left hanging around or go missing. The windows were child-friendly and would only open a little, too little for a body to pass through. So Ginny and I after discussing the situation couldn't really see where any opportunity to escape would present itself.

Nevertheless, both Ginny and I remained vigilant and kept a sharp eye on our maid and made it obvious so Mandy would realise we were monitoring her at all times. We were actually very grateful to Mandy she did make a big difference in our lives and the longer she was with us, the more dependent we became on her servitude. If she did manage to ever escape it would affect us now much more than it would have done a few months back.

The next six months went by with no problems at all and the house was beginning to look very clean, tidy and well looked after, thanks to Mandy's hard work. It wasn't all drudgery for Mandy we did give her treats. Ginny let her wear some of her dresses in the evening and we gave her time off indoors to pursue her own interests. Sometimes she would eat with us and share our wine. I also on occasion took her out for a drive in my car with the doors locked. However, one day when Ginny and I were having one of our ubiquitous chit-chat in the kitchen, Mandy came into the conversation.

"How would you feel if we took Mandy out one evening as a treat and reward for all her hard work?" Ginny asked. I thought about it for a few seconds and replied:

"What a good idea, she needs a break from all the drudgery, but do you think we can trust her now not to try and escape?" I asked.

"What do you think?" Ginny asked, "She has been very well-behaved for some time now and has not shown any signs of wanting to leave us."

"I should add," I answered, "she hasn't had much opportunity as we have been watching her like a hawk and she is shackled and can't run anywhere. If we take her out for an evening we'll have to remove all her restraints. Isn't that a little dangerous, can't we give her a treat some other way? There must be lots of nice things we can do for her without risking her escaping. I don't think we should put opportunity in her hands. "

"I don't know, she's been very well-behaved lately," Ginny replied. "Mandy would profit from a change of scenery and some real downtime. It will demonstrate to her we're not ogres and will reward good work."

"Then," I asked, "what can we do to ensure she doesn't make a run for freedom?"

"I suggest," Ginny said, that we don't let her out of our sight and if she wants to go to the toilet, one of us goes with her as well."

"Where shall we take her to," I asked, "what did you have in mind, Ginny?"

"I thought of taking her to 'The Cat and Fiddle' pub it is not far from here and there is open countryside all around, so if Mandy did escape there wouldn't be anywhere for her to go," suggested Ginny. "I also thought we could dress Mandy in something bright and colourful making her easy to spot if the pub is busy, should she want to mingle and slip away when we're not looking."

"That's a good idea," I replied. "When are you thinking of giving Mandy this treat?"

"Well, it wouldn't just be a treat for Mandy; I think we need a change too, how about tomorrow evening?"

"Yes, you need to right Ginny we a break too," I agreed. "Okay, let's do it."

Chapter Eight

We kept the surprise from Mandy and hadn't intended to let her know we were going to give her an outing until the last minute. So secretly Ginny sorted out some clothes for Mandy as she only had a maid's costume and no everyday women's wear. Fortunately, Mandy was Ginny's size. My clothes would be too small but Ginny would fit a treat and she has some nice bright and cheerful dresses to choose from. Ginny also got quite a bit of pleasure in choosing something for Mandy to wear; she had an idea of what she would like.

Mandy was still busy doing her chores when Ginny and I had her costume for the evening out sorted including some nice stiletto heels to wear instead of her boring old flats, which were already showing signs of wear from just going around and around the house and up and down the stairs numerous times a day. When I checked Mandy's housework I noticed she had missed dusting a skirting board, normally such an error would be worth a few hard strokes of my riding crop, but I didn't have the heart to punish her today, her special day out. Mandy was agog with me for letting her off punishment and was very weary as to why I had been so lenient, as I normally only needed half an excuse to bring out the cane or crop. Mandy knew how much I enjoyed spanking her and would be loath to miss an opportunity.

Mandy was also perplexed as to why we hadn't started to prepare dinner at the normal time and was probably being too worry about her own rumbling tummy. Ginny and I still didn't let on we were going to take her out to dinner tonight and allowed her to wonder what was going on and why were occasionally giving her strange looks as we mentally dressed her for her night out.

Just before 8 pm, I called Mandy up to Ginny's bedroom where we both were waiting to dress our maid for her outing. Poor Mandy didn't know what was going on and gingerly stepped into the bedroom wondering what was to become of her. I think she thought she was in for a caning or something similar.

"Come on, come in, Mandy," Ginny said cheerfully.

"Look what we have for you," I added, pointing to the clothes carefully arranged on the bed.

"For me," Mandy said faltering and confused but nonetheless relieved it wasn't a row of canes awaiting her.

"Yes Mandy, we have been so impressed with all your hard work we are going to take you out for a slap-up meal and drinks in a country pub down the road," Ginny told Mandy excitedly.

"Yes," I added, "and we can't take you out in your uniform can we, that's not on, so Ginny and I have sorted you out some nice clothes to wear for the evening."

Poor Mandy was overwhelmed and not all used to this level of kindness, not that we were ever really that horrible to her, only when she attempted to escape. "However, kindness wasn't something she could handle and began to become tearful.

"There there," Ginny said going to the dressing table to get some tissues and wiping the distraught girl's eyes. "Come on, cheer up this is a special night out in your honour; we can't take you out with red blotchy eyes, can we."

"Look at the clothes we have selected for you," I said holding up the dress. "No time to lose, the evening is escaping us, come on, strip off Mandy," I urged.

Mandy viewed the dress and the accessories on the bed and looked up at us each in turn and said:

"This is for me?"

"Yes," I said, "for you to wear tonight, not to keep, these are Ginny's clothes, but whenever we go out we'll find something nice for you to wear." This revelation had Mandy breaking down into sobs of emotion again.

Finally, we had Mandy dressed, and we quickly dressed ourselves. Mandy looked a peach in her long ankle ankle-length white floral dress, white card and black pointed stiletto heels all finished off with an ample squirt of perfume. To get us in the mood we went into the living room and had a glass of sherry each and then we went to the car outside. The sherry worked, and we were all relaxed, chatty and giggly. The drive to the pub was a short one and we parked close to the pub door. We let Mandy go first into the pub. A member of the pub staff quickly showed us to our table and brought us over a menu.

We all settled for roast chicken, roast potatoes and green beans. Ginny and I had gin and tonic and Mandy had a large glass of beer. Slowly, the pub began to fill and the atmosphere became very jovial. We allowed Mandy to drink as much as she liked and was quickly becoming quite animated as she wasn't used to alcohol. Ginny and I found her behaviour quite funny; she was so different to how we normally see her. Mandy was quite the soul of the party, and she made us laugh with her droll humour. Indeed, we were all so relaxed and enjoying ourselves, that Ginny and I quite forgot Mandy was our slave and twice we allowed her to go to the toilet without supervision.

The third time Mandy went to relieve herself was at our cost. Ginny and I were so deep in conversation that it was many minutes or even longer before either of us realised Mandy hadn't returned to the fold.

"Ginny," I said with concern tapping her arm, where is Mandy?"

"Oh she has probably gone to the loo," Ginny said emptying her glass and about to go to the bar for a refill.

"Yes," I replied, "but that was ages ago, she hasn't come back."

"Oh no," we both cried, "not again."

"What do we do," I cried.

"You go out the front and have a look around the car park and I'll go and look in the beer garden, if you can't find her meet me back here in five minutes," with these words Ginny shot off into the beer garden and I wasting no time ran for the front door. We both returned five minutes later exhausted and panting from our exertions.

"What do we do now," I asked seeing Ginny empty-handed.

"We'll look for her in the car come on," Ginny said grabbing her handbag and dragging me with her to the front door. We both climbed into her old car and I covered my ears as Ginny tore the car through the gravel making an almighty din to get to the pub entrance.

"That won't do your car paintwork any good," I observed. "Which way do you think she would have gone?" I asked.

That way goes into the deep countryside, she wouldn't have gone left. We'll drive back slowly towards the town. Keep your eyes peeled Gail," Ginny said turning the car right towards town. We drove quite slowly as both of us looked eagerly left and right.

"She could be anywhere." I said, "We don't have a hope of finding her. Mandy has done it she has got away from us this time. What if she goes straight to the police?" I asked.

"For goodness sake stop panicking," Ginny scorned, "we're only halfway back to town, we may find her yet. Mandy will stick out like a sore thumb in that white floral dress just keep your eyes peeled. Besides, I doubt if she will go to the police dressed as she is, her first thought will be getting home and as far away from us as possible."

We drove closer to the town and there was no Mandy in sight, I think we were now both getting a bit despondent as we thought we might have found her by now.

"Mandy has no money, I reckon she might have gone back to the house," Ginny offered.

"But she can't get in," I reminded Ginny.

"She can break in, can't she," Ginny replied. She must have money and she knows where we keep the household funds."

"Okay," I replied let's go and look. "We have to go home anyway eventually."

We got within two streets of the house when we saw Mandy hopping along; she had broken the heel of one of her shoes. She saw us but couldn't run, so she stopped and waited for us to pull alongside. When the car stopped, I got out and went over to Mandy.

"I am so disappointed in you Mandy," I said. "In the car now," I shouted so loud it hurt my throat. Poor Mandy quivered at the sound of my voice and almost threw herself into the back of the car. "You don't realise the trouble you are in now, my girl, just you wait until we get you indoors; you'll be in it."

As we drove the last couple of streets to the house, I looked back at a very tired and exhausted Mandy and said:

"I don't know what we are going to do with you Mandy, I really don't. We give you a nice treat and this is how you reward us. I think it is Ginny's turn to punish you this time I wash my hands on you, she's all yours Ginny." I said in frustration.

"A pleasure," Ginny said, stopping the car outside the house. "She won't want me to punish her again I will tell you."

We got out of the car and both Ginny and I held the girl's arms and frog-marched her to the front door.

Chapter Nine.

Ginny continued to drag Mandy right through the house, out of the back door and down the garden to the tool shed, there she locked Mandy in and without a single word she returned to the house rubbing her arms in satisfaction.

"She can spend the night among the hoes and spades until tomorrow morning when I am in a better mood to deal with her," Ginny said in exasperation.

"Mandy will get your dress dirty," I observed.

"Then Gail, she can scrub it until it is clean again," Ginny said quite seriously, and if she can't get it clean she will be punished for that too."

"She will also get very cold out there it is autumn, you know," I replied, "it can get very cold some nights."

"Part of the punishment," Ginny said unconcerned.

"We need to make a coffee and sit and talk about the situation," I said, knowing we needed a new strategy as ours wasn't working.

"In the morning," Ginny replied," I have had quite enough of today.

In the morning I woke to the sound of muffled screams in the garden. When I got downstairs, I looked out of the kitchen window to see Mandy in the nude, tied to a tree, despite it being nearly freezing and very early; she was getting a good beating with a willow birch. Ginny must have been punishing Mandy for a little while before I woke as her body was covered head and toe with red angry welts.

Finally, Mandy was untied from the tree and brought back to the house in chains. Mandy was given a glass of water and two pieces of mouldy bread and taken to the airing cupboard and locked in. At least the airing cupboard was warm after spending a cold night in a flimsy dress in the tool shed.

"Good," I said now Mandy is out of the way we need to talk," I said to Ginny. "Shall I put the kettle on," I added. Ginny nodded and made her way to the kitchen and sat at the kitchen table.

"Mandy has had a good spanking," Ginny said. "She won't want a repeat of this morning any time soon; I can tell you."

"Yes," I noticed," I replied.

"I don't think she'll be contemplating escaping again," Ginny assured me, "she had a very cold, sleepless night and will be sore from my administration for a couple of weeks or more."

It isn't going to work though is it?" I said. "In a few months the urge to escape will be overpowering and sooner or later she will succeed, it is only a matter of time."

"So what do you suggest we do?" Asked Ginny taking a mug of coffee from me. "We can only beat her so hard."

"We have no choice, Ginny, we shall have to let her go home," I said with resignation and disappointment in my voice.

"You know what the consequences of that might be if she goes to the police?" Ginny said. "Besides, look at all the effort we have put into taming and training, Mandy to be a good maid."

"I thought you said the police would have a hard time proving we kidnapped Mandy."

"They will," Ginny replied, "but it might not stop them from trying to make a case, it will, in either event, be weeks if not months of worry and stress for us."

"Well we don't have much of a choice unless you can think of something else," I replied passing Ginny a chocolate biscuit. "We just can't go on chasing Mandy around town every time she wants to flit."

"Poor Mandy won't be getting one of these," Ginny said mischievously taking a bite of her chocolate biscuit. She'll be enjoying two pieces of stale mouldy bread in the dark. So I presume you're suggesting, Gail, we let Mandy go and face any consequences that might follow after her release?"

"Yes," I said, "what choice do we have? We'll also be rid of the stress and worry of watching Mandy all the time which is outweighing her usefulness. I know she does a good of housekeeping, but watching her day and night takes its toll on us. Is it worth it?"

"Okay," Ginny agreed, "but she can stay in the cupboard for a while. We shall let her out for lunch and after we will tell Mandy she can leave when she is ready to go."

That was where we left matters. When lunch was ready, I went down to the airing cupboard and let a very chastised and tired maid out into the daylight and brought her back to the kitchen, flicking her bottom with my crop as we went. I unlocked her chains, gave her a hot lunch and told her to come into the living room when she had enough to eat and drink.

Around half an hour later, Mandy knocked on the open door. She stood there demurely in Ginny's now dirty dress waiting for permission to come in. Ginny and I finished our conversation and then I turned to look at Mandy.

"Come on in Mandy, I said beckoning her over to me. As Mandy approached Ginny stood and pulled up Mandy's skirt and at the same time lowered her knickers.

"You're going to be very sore for a while Mandy," Ginny said, poking one of the welts making Mandy jump and yelp at the same time.

"Come and sit down on the sofa between us, if you can," I said pointing to a spot between us on the sofa.

Mandy stepped over, gingerly sat down and glanced at me and Ginny in turn. Both Ginny and I studied Mandy for a while, which made the girl a bit jumpy as she was wondering if there was more punishment to come. Finally, to put her out of her misery I was first to speak.

"Mandy," I said in an authoritative voice, "we can't continue like this, can we, what do you have to say for yourself? Why did you try and escape yet again after so many promises not to?"

"I won't do it again, I won't try to escape again, I promise," Mandy said in a state of panic with tears welling in her eyes. "I'll be good you'll see."

"But you have said this to us before, time and time again," Ginny reminded Mandy, "and almost using the same words, how can we trust you ever again?"

"Frankly, if we are to be honest the strain of watching you night and day outweighs your usefulness, I said joining the conversation. "What are we to do?" I added. It is clear you don't wish to stay with us and Ginny and I have decided to reluctantly face reality."

"No more punishment please," Mandy begged. "I know it was wrong to run off last night, it was the alcohol that made me brazen. I just saw an opening to run away and an overwhelming urge overtook me and I took it. I hadn't gotten very far down the road when I began to regret running off, especially as you both were so kind to me, but the deed was cast so I continued to run on. I don't know what was in my mind; I had no money or plan."

"Well, Ginny and I had a long conversation about your future and we have both reluctantly come to a decision." Before I could continue Mandy began to cry and plead with me not to punish her again and that she would now behave and finally settle down as our slave.

"The decision we have made Mandy is to let you go," I said and my words had Mandy stop remonstrating and she became stunned and silent. "Yes, you may leave when you're ready, you may go and pack now if you like. You'll find your old male clothes are already on the bed together with your money and rail tickets."

"You're letting me leave. You don't want me anymore?" Mandy said not quite believing her ears. "I can go home now, today?"

"It is not a case of not wanting you anymore, indeed the opposite you have done some really good work for us in recent months," Ginny replied. "We are more than happy with your work and I might add you're a nice person and good company. I think Gail will agree we both like you."

"It's a case we cannot keep running after you every time you want to escape," I added. "The stress is making both Ginny and I ill."

"Oh Mandy," said without explanation.

"Go on then," I said you can go and pack you're free, what are you waiting for? Off you go and don't forget to message us when you get home. Also, keep in touch from time to time to let us know how you are."

"Before you go," Ginny said, interrupting as she fiddled with her handbag, "here is some extra money for food on the train," she said offering over a few bank notes. Surprisingly Mandy began to cry instead of being overwhelmed with joy.

"What if I don't want to leave?" Mandy said surprising us both. "What if I want to stay here with you both?"

"Pardon?" I replied in astonishment, looking at Ginny, who was equally flabbergasted.

"You don't want to leave?" Ginny repeated. "Can you repeat that for us both please?" Ginny asked, "Did we hear you right, or are we both dreaming?"

"No you're not dreaming, I want to stay with you both and continue as your maid," Mandy replied looking very concerned as she mopped her tears away.

This revelation caused several moments of complete silence as Ginny and I grappled with what Mandy was implying. Now everything has been turned on its head and nothing was making very much sense.

"Now," I said breaking the silence. "Let's get this straight. You want to voluntarily stay with us as our slave and maid?

"Yes please," Mandy replied with a nod to reinforce her reply.

"Then, pray tell us why you have spent so much time and effort trying to escape and go home?"

Ginny said in exasperation. "It simply doesn't make any sense, please explain to us both."

"I acted the way I did because you were forcing me to stay against my will," Mandy replied quite forcefully. "I didn't like being forced to be your maid. That was one choice I thought I should be allowed to make."

"You mean to say, if we asked you nicely to stay and be our maid, you would have said yes and it would have saved us months and months of grief," I said in total astonishment.

"Not for the first couple of weeks I was very angry with you. I did want to leave and looked for every opportunity to go, but after a while, I settled in a bit more, got into a routine and began to enjoy my work. Yes, I would have been happy to stay, but I wanted the decision to be mine, not yours. I wanted that one say to be mine," Mandy explained. "It was important that

I alone made that one crucial decision about my future."

"Astonishing," Ginny replied, not quite believing her ears. So let's get this straight once and for all. If we were to ask you now to stay and be our maid what would you say? It will be a life of menial work, seven days a week, no holidays and no prospect of a pension; you would say yes."

"And no more running away," I added interrupting.

"Yes," Mandy repeated. "Yes, I would stay and become your property, but it would be my choice and not thrust on me against my will."

"Then Mandy, I will ask you this one question, but before you answer I want you to give it some serious thought, if you need it you can go to your bedroom and think about it for an hour and return to give us your reply. The question is; will you stay and be our maid for life?" I asked.

"Yes please," Mandy replied without any hesitation. Ginny and I looked at each other again quite perplexed and bewildered.

"Then go and put the kettle on Mandy, we'll have a celebratory cup of tea and a currant bun and then after a break, you may go back to work," Ginny said pointing to the kettle.

And so it was. Mandy became a compliant, gentle loyal maid and was never any trouble to us again. Although Mandy was our slave not paid and had no pension plan, she, however, became a truly valued member of our family and was treated as such and wanted for nothing.

The End

Check out my other books:

The Chronicles of a Male Slave.

A real-life account of a consensual slave. The book follows the life of an individual who comes to terms with his submissive side, his search for a Mistress and his subsequent experiences as a consensual slave.
This book gives a real insight into the B.D.S.M. lifestyle and what it is like to be a real slave to a lifestyle Mistress.

Mistress Margaret.

This is the story of young teenage boy Brenden, who is finding out about his sexuality when he meets older Mistress Margaret a nonprofessional dominatrix. Mistress Margaret takes Brenden's hand and shows him the mysterious, erotic world of BDSM and all it has to offer.

The week that changed my life.

A tale about a young girl discovering her sexuality with an older, more mature dominant man whilst on a week's holiday by the sea. She was introduced into a world of BDSM that would change her outlook on life forever.

The Temple of Gor.

Hidden in the wilds of Scotland is The Temple of Gor, a secret B.D.S.M., society. In the Temple, you will find Masters and their female slaves living in a shared commune. The community is based on the Gorean subculture depicted in a fictional novel by John Norman and has taken a step too far and turned into a macabre reality. Stella a young girl from England, stumbles on the commune and is captured and turned into a Kajira slave girl until she finds a way to escape her captors.

Becoming a Sissy Maid.

This is a true story of one person's quest to become a sissy maid for a dominant couple. The story outlines the correspondence between the Master, Mistress, and sissy maid, that leads up to their first and second real-time meeting.

It is a fascinating tale and is a true, honest and accurate account, only the names and places have been changed to protect the individuals involved. It is a must-be-read book by anyone into BDSM and will give an interesting insight for anyone wishing to become in the future a real-time sissy maid.

Meet Maisy The Sissy Maid.

This story is about Maisy a sissy maid and her life. The story takes Maisy through all the various stages a sissy has to make take to find her true submissive and feminine self. It is a long and arduous road and many transitions before Maisy finds true happiness as a lady's maid for her Mistress.

Beginner's Guide For The Serious Sissy
Best selling

So you want to be a woman and dress and behave like a sissy? You accept you cannot compete with most men and now want to try something new and different. This guide will help you along the way and walk the potential sissy through the advantages and pitfalls of living as a submissive woman.

Becoming a serious sissy requires making changes that are both physical and mental. This will involve learning to cross-dress, leg-crossing, sit, stand, bend hair removal, wear makeup, use cosmetics, and sit down to pee.

You'll learn feminine mannerisms such as stepping daintily, arching your spine, swishing your hips, and adopting a feminine voice. You'll understand more about hormone treatment and herbal supplements.

There is advice and tips on going out in public for the first time and coming out of the closet to friends, colleagues, and family. The guide will help you to slowly lose your masculine identity and replace it with a softer gentler feminine one.

A collaring for a sissy.

Collaring ceremonies are taken very seriously by the B.D.S.M., community and are tantamount to a traditional wedding. Lots of thought and planning go into such an event and can take many forms.

Mistress Anastasia's sissy maid Paula has just completed her six months probation and has earned her collar. This is a story about Paula's service and her subsequent collaring ceremony.

The secret society.

Rene Glock is a freelance journalist looking for a national scoop and attempts to uncover and expose a Secret Society of Goreans which have set up residence in an old nightclub. However, as he delves into the secret world he finds he has an interest in BDSM and questions his moral right to interfere in what goes on in the Gorean Lodge.

The Good Master and Mistress Guide.

If you want to become a good Dominant and practice B.D.S.M., in a safe and considerate way, then this guide is for you.

It is written by a submissive who has had many dominants male and female over the years and knows what goes into becoming a good dominant and the mistakes some dominants make.

The book is not aimed to teach, but to make the fledgling dominant understand what is going on in the dominant-submissive dynamic, so they can understand their charges better and become better dominants.

My Transgender Journey

This is a true story with some minor alterations to protect people's identities. It is a tale about my own journey into transgender and my eventual decision to come out.

It is hoped that others can share my experiences relate to them and perhaps take comfort from some of them.

The book has some BDSM content but is only used to put my story into context, it's about my experiences, trials and tribulations of coming out and living as a female full-time.

I hope you enjoy my little story.

Cinders

Cinders is the BDSM version of Cinderella. It is a story where an orphaned Tommy is sent to be brought up by his aunt and two very beautiful sisters.

The sisters were cruel and taunting and dressed Tommy up like a Barbie Doll. One day Tommy is caught with Auntie's bra and knickers and as a punishment, he is feminised and turned into Nancy the maid. Poor Nancy is consigned to a life of drudgery and final acceptance of life as a menial skivvy.

This story doesn't have a glass slipper or a prince, but Nancy is given a present of some new rubber gloves and a bottle of bleach. There is no happy ending or is there, you decide.

At the races

Ryan is a hotel night porter and is at a crossroads in his life. He feels his talents are being wasted in a job with no future. Through a friend, he is offered a managerial position on a farm in Catalonia, Spain. He decides to take the post but has no idea what sort of farm he is going to work at.

Only on the flight out to Spain does Ryan realise that there is more to the farm than rearing chickens and growing vegetables. Later he learns the main event of the year is The Derby and there isn't a horse in sight.

I nearly married a Dominatrix

This is a true story that I have changed a little bit to protect people from identification. It's a story about a man's constant struggle and fight against his deep-rooted need to be submissive and a woman who conversely, is very comfortable with her dominance and heavily into the BDSM lifestyle.

They meet and get along very well indeed until Mistress Fiona announces she wants to become a professional dominatrix. Rex, the submissive boyfriend goes along with his Mistress's plans, reluctantly, but as time goes by there are more and more complications heaped on the relationship until it snaps.

Be careful what you ask for

There is an old English adage: Be careful about what you ask for; it may come true.

This is a story about a B.D.S.M., fantasy that has gone badly wrong.

Fantasy is simply a fantasy and we all have them regardless of our sexuality. Fantasies are quite harmless until we choose to act them out for real and when do act out our fantasies the line between fantasy and reality can become very blurred. This is a tale about one person's fantasy that becomes all too real for comfort.

Petticoat Lane.

A slightly effeminate young boy is taken under the wings of his school teacher. She becomes his guardian and trains him to become a servant girl to serve her for the rest of his life.

An unexpected incident happens and Lucy the maid has an opportunity to escape her life of drudgery and servitude, but does she take the opportunity or does she stay with her Mistress?

The life and times of a Victorian maid.

This is a story about the life and times of a young Transgender who becomes a Victorian-style maid in a large exclusively B.D.S.M., household. Although fiction this story is largely based on fact, as the author herself lived in such a household for a while as a maid.

It shows the contrast between a place of safety where like-minded people can live in relative harmony and the need for ridged discipline in its serving staff.

There are many thriving households, such as the one mentioned here, tucked away out of sight and away from prying minds.

I became a kajira slave girl.

A Gorean scout Simon, who is looking for new talent kidnaps Emma a PhD student on sabbatical with her friend Zoey in Spain. Emma is half-drugged and sent across the ocean to the United States and ends up in the clandestine

City of Gor in the Mojave desert sixty miles from civilization.

Here there is no law women are mere objects for the pleasure of men. Emma becomes a Kajira a female slave whose sole purpose in life is to please her master or be beaten tortured or killed.

Two years into Emma's servitude she meets Simon again. Simon is consumed with guilt when he sees what Emma has been reduced to, a beaten, downtrodden and abused slave. He vows to free her from her servitude, But how they are in one of the biggest deserts in the world and sixty miles from anywhere?

Training my first sissy maid.

A young single mother with a part-time job, two teenage children, and up to her knees in housework is at the end of her tether and finding it harder and harder to cope.

Then reading one of her daughter's kinky magazines she found in her bedroom whilst tidying, read an article about sissy maids who are willing to work without pay just for discipline, control and structure to their lives. Excited about the prospect she decides a maid is an answer to her domestic problems.

She sets about finding a sissy to come and do her housework and be trained and moulded into becoming her loyal obedient sissy maid. On the journey, she discovers she is a natural dominant and training her maid becomes a highly erotic and fulfilling experience.

A week with Mistress Sadistic.

Susan a young female reporter in her thirties wants to know more about B.D.S.M., for a future article in her magazine. She arranged to spend a week with Mistress Sadistic and watch how a professional dominatrix works.

After an eye-opening week of watching Mistress Sadistic deal with her many and varied clients, Mistress Sadistic wonders if Susan might be submissive and puts her to the text to make Susan her personal slave.

Lady Frobisher and her maid Alice.

This is a gripping tale of B.D.SM., in Victorian England. It is a story about the lives of Lady Frobisher and her hapless maid Alice. It is a tale of lesbianism and sexual sadism with a twist at the end.

If you enjoy reading B.D.S.M., literature you'll love this as it has everything woven into an interesting tale of two people's lives at the top end of society.

K9

This is a tale that explores an area of B.D.S.M., where a Mistress or Master desires a human dog (submissive) to be trained and treated as a real dog in every respect. Mistress Cruella is one such Mistress who takes on a young male submissive as her human dog and she takes the role of Mistress and her dog very seriously indeed.

Ryan soon becomes Max the Poodle and he struggles with his new role as a pooch but learns to be an obedient dog to please his Mistress. Max soon discovers there is far more to being a dog than meets the eye.

Bridget Monroe's Finishing School for Sissies.

Bridget and her husband are both dominant and have their own sissy maid Isabel to help them with housework. One day when the couple were on holiday in Kent, Bridget discovered an empty manor house in need of extensive repairs. On inquires, she decides to buy the manor but soon realises that to pay for the mortgage and repair costs the manor house will need to be run as a business.

Bridget used willing slaves in the B.D.S.M., community to help repair and renovate the manor house and later it was decided on advice from friends to open the manor house as a finishing school for sissies. A business had been born and later other B.D.S.M., activities were added to the core business, which included torture rooms and a medieval dungeon. Once a month an open day was held at the academy and there were pony races, yard sales and schoolboy classes. This also included K9 dog shows, beer tents and other amenities intending to satisfy the whole B.D.S.M., community.

Just when the business was taking off and in profit, disaster struck. Society wasn't ready for

Bridget Monroe's Finishing School for Sissies and Bridget was forced to close.

The girl with the faraway eyes.
Recommended

This is a tale of stalking between a probation psychologist and one of his female self-harming clients, who is about to appear in court for habitual shoplifting and running the risk of a custodial sentence.

A series of innocent appointments arranged to provide the courts with background information leads to the young, impressionable client forming a submissive (B.D.S.M.,) sexual attachment to her old psychologist. The psychologist out of kindness and concern for the girl inadvertently makes the situation far worse.

This is a gripping tale of unrequited love which becomes highly destructive and gathers pace and finally tears both their lives apart and nearly destroys the life of a young girl and a psychologist's career.

Everything you wanted to know about Gor, but was afraid to ask.

The Gor Novels by John Norton have been the fascination of many in the B.D.S.M., scene. Unless you're a fan of the novels, you're not likely to know very much about the Gorean lifestyle.

This book will demystify the culture and explain how the cult works. It will show how the culture transcended from just fictional novels to the chat room and for some into everyday life.

This book isn't exhaustive because the culture is in a state of flux and forever changing and moving away from the novels and morphing into a culture all of its own.

There have recently been several criminal proceedings against Gor cult followers. Many B.D.S.M., practitioners think that Gor is a step too far and departs from the guiding principle in B.D.S.M., and that all play should be consensual and agreed upon. What do you think?

I became a sissy to escape the draft

During the 1950s National Military Service was imposed on young men between the ages of 18 and 24. Perhaps not too surprisingly not everybody was keen to give up two years of their lives serving their country.

Many such young men skipped the country or were hidden away at home in the cellar or false compartments. One such young man who wanted to escape not only the draft, but the Korean War took more drastic measures and with the help of his dominant Auntie was forced by circumstances to become a woman to avoid detection by the authorities. Lucy as she came to be known had given up one form of incarceration and discipline for another and was slowly reduced to becoming Auntie's maid and servant.

Petticoat punishment for unruly boys

This is a tale of the effective petticoat punishments that were meted out at some schools in England in the 1950s. It was often a punishment preferred to corporal punishment which was slowly becoming unpopular and used less and less in British schools and was outlawed completely by the 1980s.

This is one such story of a man who endured petticoat punishment when he was eight or nine years old and how it had a profound psychological effect on him and changed his life forever.

Printed in Great Britain
by Amazon

38876808R00089